ONE HUNDRED HUNGRY ANTS

BY ELINOR J. PINCZES
ILLUSTRATED BY BONNIE MACKAIN

Houghton Mifflin Company Boston

Special thanks to Katie, my daughter, and Casey, my granddaughter, for their inspiration.—E.P.

For my parents, with love—B.S.M.

Text copyright © 1993 by Elinor J. Pinczes
Illustrations copyright © 1993 by Bonnie MacKain

Library of Congress Cataloging-in-Publication Data

Pinczes, Elinor J.
  One hundred hungry ants / Elinor J. Pinczes ; illustrated by
Bonnie MacKain.
    p. cm.
  Summary: One hundred hungry ants head towards a picnic to
get yummies for their tummies, but stops to change their line
formation, showing different divisions of 100, cause them to lose
both time and food in the end.
    RNF ISBN 0-395-63116-5   PAP ISBN 0-395-97123-3
    [1. Ants—Fiction. 2. Stories in rhyme. 3. Division.]
I. MacKain, Bonnie, ill. II. Title. III. Title: 100 hungry ants.
PZ8.3.P5586760n 1993   91-45415
[E]—dc20   CIP
                  AC

Manufactured in China
LEO 40 39 38 37 36 35
4500341851

A whole hill of hungry ants,
their faces all aglow,
came swarming from the forest
to cross the field below.

A soft breeze fanned the sunshine
and whisked them on their way.
It hinted of yummies
for their empty tummies—
that means a picnic! Hooray!

One hundred ants were singing
and marching in a row.

"We're going to a picnic!
A hey and a hi dee ho!"

"Stop," said the littlest ant.
"We're moving way too slow.
Some food will be long gone
unless we hurry up. So . . .

with 2 lines of 50
we'd get there soon, I know."

All the ants raced here and there,
up, down, and to and fro.

"There'll be lots of yummies
for our hungry tummies,
A hey and a hi dee ho!"

One hundred ants were singing
and marching in 2 rows.

"We're going to a picnic!
A hey and a hi dee ho!"

"Stop!" yelled the littlest ant.
"We're moving way too slow!
More of the food will be gone
unless we hurry up. So . . .
with 4 lines of 25
we'd get there soon, I know."

All the ants raced here and there,
up, down, and to and fro.
"We hope there's yummies
for our rumbling tummies,
A hey and a hi dee ho!"

One hundred ants were singing
and marching in 4 rows.

"We're going to a picnic!
A hey and a hi dee ho!"

"Stop!" screamed the littlest ant.
"We're moving way too slow!
Lots of food will long be gone
unless we hurry up. So . . .
with 5 lines of 20
we'd get there soon, I know."

All the ants raced here and there,
up, down, and to and fro.
"There might be a yummy
for a gurgling tummy,
A hey and a hi dee ho!"

One hundred ants were singing
and marching in 5 rows.

"We're going to a picnic!
A hey and a hi dee ho!"

"Stop!" shrieked the littlest ant.
"We're moving way too slow!
All the food will long be gone
unless we hurry up. So . . .
with 10 lines of 10
we'd get there soon, I know."

All the ants raced here and there,
up, down, and to and fro.
"There better be yummies
for our grumbling tummies,
A hey and a hi dee ho!"

One hundred ants were singing
and marching in 10 rows.

"At last, we're at the picnic!
A hey and a hi dee ho!"

"Stop!" yipped the littlest ant.
"We've traveled way too slow!

There's no food for us to eat,
you took so long with rows."

All the ants raced here and there,
up, down, and to and fro.
"There aren't any yummies
for our growling tummies?
A hey and a hi dee ho!

OH! NO!"

Ninety-nine ants were swarming
from each and every row,
in hot pursuit of one little ant,
who quickly turned to go.

"It's not all my fault, you know!"

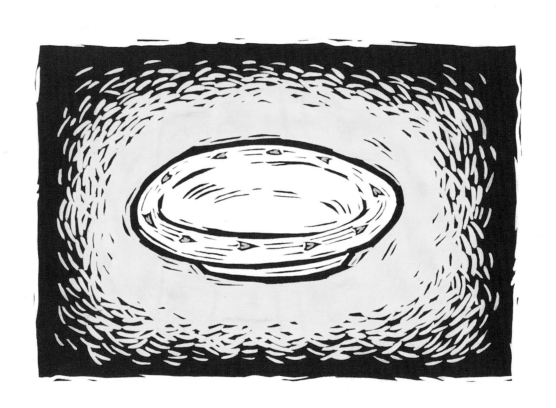